Theft at
George Eastman House

Sally Valentine

A New York State Adventure

Theft at George Eastman House

ISBN-10 1-59531-029-0
ISBN-13 978-1-59531-029-3

Illustrations by Martha Gulley
Design by Zach Steffen & Rob Igoe, Jr.

Library of Congress Cataloging-in-Publication Data

Valentine, Sally.
  Theft at George Eastman house / [by Sally Valentine].
     p. cm.
  Summary: Students from a Rochester, New York, elementary school
learn about photography and the steps in solving a mystery when a
valuable candlestick is stolen during their field trip to the George
Eastman House museum.
  ISBN-13: 978-1-59531-029-3 (alk. paper)
  ISBN-10: 1-59531-029-0 (alk. paper)
  [1. Photography--Fiction. 2. Mystery and detective stories. 3. George
Eastman House--Fiction. 4. Schools--Fiction. 5. Rochester (N.Y.)--
Fiction.] I. Title.
  PZ7.V25215The 2009
  [Fic]--dc22
                                        2009007904

North Country Books, Inc
220 Lafayette Street
Utica, New York 13502
www.northcountrybooks.com

To Shelly,

*I hope this inspires you
to promote your own writing.
Anything is possible . . .*

Love,
Sally 7/4/09

This book is dedicated to the children in the
city of Rochester, New York. May you love
your hometown like George Eastman did,
and may you never stop asking questions.

Chapter 1

"Smile!" Click. Flash.

"Smile!" Click. Flash.

"Smile!" Click. Flash.

Mrs. Levine surprised the first three students who walked through the classroom door by taking their pictures.

"Smile!" Click. Flash.

"Smile!" Click. Flash.

Two more students blinked at the flash as they walked past the Welcome to Fifth Grade sign and into Room 217 of Susan B. Anthony School #27. Until last June Mrs. Levine had always taught fourth grade, but Mr. Coley, the school principal, moved her up one grade when Mrs. Levine's fourth grade students gained notoriety by rescuing the Charlotte Lighthouse.

The whole class had raised money to refurbish the run-down lighthouse, and a particular group of students, who called themselves The STARfish, had found ten shares of stock in the Eastman Dry Plate and Film Company holed up in the lighthouse tower wall. The stock, from the company that is now called Eastman

Kodak, turned out to be worth a bundle.

Mr. Levine, Mrs. Levine's lawyer husband, determined that the money belonged to Miss Brenda Robinson, the great-great-great-niece of lighthouse keeper Cuyler Cook. Miss Robinson, who lived in a nursing home in Kalamazoo, Michigan, used some of the money to finish restoring the lighthouse. She also rewarded the students with a state of the art computer system, including an ink-jet printer and lots of software. Mr. Coley thought it only right that Mrs. Levine be promoted to fifth grade along with her class, so they could all benefit from the generous gift together. The only problem was that Mrs. Levine wasn't so sure that she would like this gift as much as the children would. Mrs. Levine was some-what of an old-fashioned teacher. She could go along with some new educational ideas like cooperative learning and even the new math, but she liked books better than computers.

"Smile!" Click. Flash.

"Smile!" Click. Flash.

"Smile!" Click. Flash.

The next group of unsuspecting students was photo-graphed upon entering. A loud "Whooo! Whooo!" followed each click and flash as the already assembled students greeted each new arrival with enthusiasm.

In less than an hour, all twenty-two students had been photographed and assigned a desk and a cubby, and Mrs. Levine was inwardly congratulating herself on a smooth opening to the new school year.

"This will be a great year, class," she said, as she

went to the chalkboard. With a brand new piece of chalk, she wrote the date, September 8, 1999, in big letters across the clean green surface, wincing only a little bit inside at the change from black chalkboards to green. Then she looked at some of her students from last year—Janie, Jeanetta, Lamar, Reinaldo, and Derrick, who made up The STARfish. They were all sitting in the first row across.

"Mrs. Levine must have put us up here because she likes us best," whispered Reinaldo to Lamar, who was seated to his right. Actually, after the events of last year, Mrs. Levine had put them directly in front of her so that she could keep an eye on them at all times.

"I'm sure you noticed," began Mrs. Levine, "that some of our friends are gone. Felicia went to live with her dad in Florida, Tawanda moved across town, and I don't know what happened to Rodney. Luckily, we have five new students to replace them. I'd like you all to welcome Cassandra Gray from Alabama, Terry Watkins from #43 School, Leroy Dickerson from #4 School, Jazmin Garcia from Puerto Rico, and Tonya Peterson from #52 School." Each new student waved shyly as his or her name was called, and each got hesitant smiles from his or her classmates in return.

"Welcome, new students," said Mrs. Levine. "As you know, this is a charter school that specializes in cooperative learning, and you will have many opportunities to get to know your classmates as you work together this year. We all work very hard to get along with each other here." As she said this, she looked at Derrick and Janie, who had not always gotten along so well last year.

"Is that why you took our pictures, Mrs. Levine, because we have so many new kids?" interrupted Tomas.

"I'm glad you're still full of questions, Tomas. Actually, I took the pictures to introduce you to photography, which is our new unit of study this year. Because The STARfish discovered the hidden Eastman Kodak Co. stock last year, I thought it would be fun to learn more about George Eastman and photography. We'll be learning how to take pictures and develop them, and we'll even visit Mr. Eastman's house."

"Where does Mr. Eastman live?" asked Debra.

"Mr. Eastman's dead, stupid," said Derrick.

Mrs. Levine let out the first sigh of the year. Long ago Mrs. Levine had gotten the reputation as the best sigher in all of School #27. In fact, unkind people were given to rating her sighs on a scale of one to ten. This sigh was only a two. Usually the sighs that rated nines and tens didn't appear until May or June.

"Let's not start the year by name-calling, Derrick. Please apologize to Debra."

"I'm sorry you're stupid, Debra," said Derrick. After a thunderous look from Mrs. Levine, he quickly amended that to, "I'm sorry I called you stupid, Debra."

Mrs. Levine's eyes did not leave Derrick's face as she continued. "Now to answer your question, Debra, I have to admit that Derrick is correct, although he expressed himself poorly. Mr. Eastman died in 1932, but the home he built on East Avenue is open to the public for tours. His property also houses the

International Museum of Photography and Film. Remember when Mayor Johnson cut the ribbon to reopen the Charlotte Lighthouse after it had been refurbished? Well, the same thing happened to the Eastman House in 1949, but they cut a strip of film instead of ribbon when it re-opened."

"What did George Eastman do, anyway?" asked Anthony.

"He invented photography," answered Donald.

"No, he didn't. He invented the camera," said Maria.

"Actually, you're both wrong," corrected Mrs. Levine. "A form of photography has been around since the Greeks and Romans ruled the ancient world, and the modern camera was invented by Jacques Daguerre of France." She went to the chalkboard and wrote that name as well as George Eastman's under the date. "George Eastman is important because he changed photography from a special skill needing lots of awkward equipment to a process that anyone can do."

"As a young man George Eastman worked at the Rochester Savings Bank, but he wanted to take a vacation to Santo Domingo. His friends told him to take lots of pictures on the trip, but when he found out how much equipment he would have to take and how much that equipment would cost, he decided not to go. Instead, he learned everything he could about photography and became determined to find a better and easier way to do it. We'll learn a lot about Mr. Eastman this year."

Chapter 2

By the next morning, Mrs. Levine had a photograph of each student taped to his or her cubby and a copy at each desk to take home to share with parents. Right away the complaining started. Brian thought his picture made him look nerdy. Derrick thought his ears looked too big. Terry didn't like the shirt his mother made him wear. On and on it went. Only Lamar was satisfied, saying, "I guess it looks like me."

"Where's your picture, Mrs. Levine?" asked Tomas.

"I was afraid you'd ask me that. I knew it wouldn't be fair to take your pictures and not take one of myself, so I had Mr. Coley snap one of me at my desk. Unfortunately, I had to sneeze just as the flash went off, and it was the last shot on the roll." Hesitantly, she brought out her own photo. With eyes half closed and fingers up to her nose, she looked like an ad for hay fever medicine. The first giggle came from the back of the room, but soon everyone, including Mrs. Levine, joined in the laughter.

"I guess my picture's not so bad after all," said Derrick as many heads nodded in agreement.

"You've got to put it on your desk," said Brian.

"Yeah," everyone else chimed in. So Mrs. Levine very slowly and dramatically got out the masking tape and affixed her new portrait to her metal desk.

"No, no, not on the side of the desk facing you," said Derrick. "Put it on this side, so that everyone who walks in will see it." Reluctantly, Mrs. Levine moved the picture, and another day in Room 217 of Susan B. Anthony School #27 had begun.

"When do we get our cameras?" asked Janie as they returned to the classroom after lunch. So far the class had read only one story, worked on two pages of math, and copied their new spelling words off the board. They had done no science or social studies at all, but already Janie was looking for a distraction from seatwork.

"I didn't promise you cameras, did I?" responded Mrs. Levine.

"Well, you said we'd be learning about photography."

"And so we will, but you're not ready for real cameras yet. We need to start at the beginning. Did you know that in order to take pictures you need both light and darkness? In fact, the word photography means writing with light, and the word camera comes from the Latin words *camera obscura*, which mean dark chamber. She wrote the words light, darkness, *camera obscura*, and dark chamber on the board. The difference between lightness and darkness is called contrast. Who knows what the oldest light in the world is?"

"Lanterns."

"Candles."

"Fire."

"The sun."

Mrs. Levine smiled at the last answer. "Jeanetta, you're right as usual. The sun is the oldest light in the world, so that's why we're going to start our unit on photography by making sun prints." Mrs. Levine went on to explain that sun prints were made by putting opaque objects on paper that had been treated with a chemical emulsion. Then the paper was put out in the sun to develop. The light from the sun would turn the light paper dark and the area under the dark objects light. Light becomes dark and dark becomes light.

"But Mrs. Levine, what if the sun never shines again?" complained Janie as she glanced over at the classroom windows, which had stripes of water running down them. It had been raining since Sunday.

"Think positively. The sun will come out eventually, and meanwhile that will give us time to collect and assemble our opaque objects. Everyone will make two sun prints. The first will have objects of your own choosing, and the second will be pictures of leaves, which the others will have to identify."

The students were excited as they left for the day, eager to search their homes for interesting objects that were small enough to fit on the special six by nine inch photo paper. Jeanneta assembled a group of hair accessories—beads, rubber bands, a pick, and pieces of ribbon. Reinaldo raided his mother's pantry and came in with all different types of pasta. He even had the name of each type written down and spelled correctly.

Janie used her father's beer bottle caps and toothpicks to make flower designs. Mrs. Levine was very pleased with the creativity that her students had shown in collecting objects—that is, she was pleased until the phone rang.

Chapter 3

The room went silent as the students listened in on Mrs. Levine's end of the conversation.

"Why, yes, Mrs. Davis, I asked the class to bring in a collection of objects to use for making sun prints."

"Could you speak a little louder, Mrs. Davis? I'm having trouble hearing you over the crying in the background. One of Derrick's little brothers must be upset."

"I'm sorry, Mrs. Davis. I assumed that Derrick's collection of toy wheels had come from old and broken toys or Legos. I had no idea he had taken them from Louis and Richard's toy trucks. No wonder they're crying." These last sentences were spoken while glaring at Derrick, who sank lower in his seat with each word.

"Of course I'll put Derrick on so that you can speak to him yourself."

All eyes were on Derrick as he slunk over to the phone.

"But, Mom, I was only borrowing the wheels. I was gonna put them back."

The rest of the class didn't have to strain to hear Mrs. Davis' voice coming loud and clear through the phone receiver. She even drowned out the sound of the younger boys' crying.

"DERRICK DAVIS, YOU BRING THOSE WHEELS HOME RIGHT AFTER SCHOOL, AND DON'T PLAN ON GOING ANYWHERE FOR THE REST OF THE WEEK!"

Derrick turned as he hung up the phone and caught the tail end of one of Mrs. Levine's sighs. Two sighs this year and they had both been caused by Derrick.

"Derrick, you will not participate in making this sun print, but I think I will leave the rest of the punishment to your mother. It sounds like she's mad enough for the both of us."

"But I was gonna put them back," mumbled Derrick again as he slunk back to his seat.

Of course, Mrs. Levine could not pass up this opportunity to lecture the class about taking other people's property without permission. Derrick thought about his theory that teachers got paid an extra $100 whenever they lectured their students. Mrs. Levine must be getting rich off of me, he thought, as he tried to close his ears to the drone of her voice.

Chapter 4

The sun finally shone on Friday, and the class (except for Derrick) very slowly and carefully carried their opaque arrangements outside to the east side of the school. Although Lamar had offered to share his sun print with Derrick, Mrs. Levine insisted that Derrick spend some quality time with Mr. Coley, the school principal. Each student's photographic paper was set inside a shirt box lid for ease of carrying. When the boxes were safely set in place, Mrs. Levine left Jeanetta to guard them and motioned the others to follow her. Not being one to waste time, Mrs. Levine pulled out a garbage bag and led the class on a march around the school grounds picking up litter. "Many hands make light work, I always say."

Mrs. Levine always says a lot of things, thought Janie.

It seemed that they had only just gotten started when Jeanetta called them to announce that the sun prints were ready. Everyone ran to retrieve his or her box.

"You are all now officially photographers," pronounced Mrs. Levine as she proudly watched her students excitedly admire each other's work. The rest of the afternoon was spent making frames, mounting the creative designs, and talking about the next set of sun prints.

"Remember, your next set of prints must relate to science. I want you to look for the most unusual kind of leaf you can find and look up its common name and its scientific name. The leaf can be from a tree or a plant."

"I will give you photographic paper to make the print of your leaf at home. You will bring the sun print and the leaf, hidden in an envelope, back to school by next Friday."

"Then we will have a contest. The student who correctly identifies the most leaves from the prints will win a prize. And the person who bests stumps the class with the most unusual leaf will also win a prize.

"A word of caution. You may pick up any leaf on the sidewalk, but DO NOT trespass into someone else's yard looking for leaves. If you see an interesting plant or tree in a neighbor's yard, ring the doorbell and ask for permission to take a leaf. Remember, taking something from someone else, even if it's only a leaf, is stealing. Have I made myself clear?" These last words were spoken while looking at each one of The STARfish in turn.

"Can Derrick work on this sun print?" asked Lamar for his friend. Derrick didn't think to ask for himself because his mind was on the extra $100 that Mrs. Levine was probably earning for another lecture on stealing.

"I guess Derrick can participate, but I will be speaking to his mother first."

Bobby went right home and picked an orange maple

leaf off the sidewalk to use for his sun print. He didn't care that it was probably the most common leaf in western New York. He liked the color and the shape. It was a bit wrinkled, but he knew that his mom would help him iron it flat so it would make a good print.

Debra went directly to her mother's garden where she grew fresh herbs. She looked carefully at the thyme, oregano, and chives that were growing there but finally settled on basil leaves. Mrs. Levine had said that if the leaves were small, they should print a whole branch, and that's what she decided to do.

Derrick, Lamar, and Reinaldo decided to look for their leaves in the vacant lot on the corner of Bay and Sixth Streets that they passed every day on their walk home from school. They figured Mrs. Levine couldn't complain about them trespassing on an empty lot.

"Aren't we supposed to keep our leaves secret from each other?" remembered Lamar as he reached down to pick up some dandelion leaves. The shape of the dandelion leaves reminded him of feathers.

"Aw, who's gonna know?" said Derrick. "If I don't tell, and you don't tell, and Reinaldo don't tell, no one will know. Mrs. Levine will just think that we're naturally smart when we figure out each other's answers."

The three agreed, and Derrick reached up to pick some leaves from a wild grape vine that had wrapped itself around the trunk of a tree. He put a half-dozen leaves inside the cover of his math book to keep them flat. It was the first time he had opened his math book that year.

Reinaldo found another vine that was reddish. He liked the way the leaves were grouped in threes. "What's that?" Derrick wanted to know.

"I don't know, but I like it, and I'll look it up in our reference books at school." He took it right home to show his little sister Maria. Maria was only sixteen months old, but Reinaldo always showed Maria his schoolwork when he got home in the afternoon. He would read Maria his essays and try to get her to do simple math on her fingers. Usually Maria wasn't interested in schoolwork, but Maria loved her big brother and she would love these leaves.

Jeanetta and Janie were also discussing the leaf print project on their way home. They wanted to do their project together like they did almost everything together, but Mrs. Levine told them to keep it a secret even from their friends. Janie and Jeanetta had been best friends since second grade, when they had both fallen off the school bus into the same mud puddle. Jeanetta did tell Janie that she was going to look for some leaves on her mother's houseplants. Mrs. Jones loved flowers and had lots of plants to choose from. Jeanetta was sure that she could find something very unusual. After all, Mrs. Levine had not said that it had to be an outdoor leaf.

Janie was still thinking about where she would get an unusual leaf as she walked up her porch steps. She let herself into the upstairs apartment of the double house where she lived with her dad. As usual, she shouted hello to Mrs. Battaglia, who lived downstairs. Janie's mom had died when she was an infant, and until this year Janie had stayed downstairs with Mrs. Battaglia after school. Now that she had turned ten, Janie convinced her dad that she was old enough to carry her own key and stay alone when she got home from school. Her dad reluctantly agreed, on the condition that she stay inside, lock the door, and call him at work just as soon as she got home.

After Janie's mother died, her Grandma Washburn had taken charge of fixing up Janie's bedroom. Grandma had seen to it that Janie got a white canopy bed with a dresser and desk to match. The bedspread, canopy, and matching tied-back curtains were all sewn from pink and white checked material and trimmed with white eyelet. Even the lampshade was pink and white. Janie didn't have the heart to tell Grandma she'd rather have bunk beds and denim curtains, so for now she lived in the frilly room she called The Palace.

To get to The Palace, Janie had to walk through the living room with its hand-me-down furniture and worn out rug. Janie's mom and dad had planned to replace the furniture when they could afford it, but when his wife died, Glenn Washburn lost interest in furniture. The only new item in the room was the 35" big screen TV that Glenn treated himself to when he turned thirty several years ago. Grandma Washburn had tried to add some feminine touches to this room, too, but gave up when Glenn hung three NASCAR posters over the couch.

As she gazed out the window past the end table with the tattered doily and her forgotten lunch money on it, Janie had an idea. Jeanetta's words kept running around in her mind. "Mrs. Levine didn't say it had to be an outdoor leaf." Janie punched her father's work number into the cordless phone as she started down the hall to The Palace. She mumbled to herself, "Best friend or not, I'm not going to let Jeanetta win this contest."

Chapter 5

Monday morning in Room 217 began uneventfully, as Mondays usually did. Only Reinaldo was acting restless. He just couldn't seem to get comfortable in his chair. Mrs. Levine found that on Monday mornings she could whip right through even the most boring reading and language arts lessons in no time at all. Then it was on to math and lunch before anyone was fully awake and ready to argue.

So the room was especially quiet, and when the phone rang, it jolted everyone to attention. Everyone, that is, except Derrick, who slunk down in his seat. I hope its not someone complaining about something I've done wrong, he thought. He breathed a sigh of relief and sat up straight again when he heard Mrs. Levine's end of the conversation.

"Why, good morning, Mrs. Santiago. How nice of you to call. Yes, the students were supposed to find leaves to make sun prints with. Reinaldo didn't cut the leaf off your prized African violet did he?" She gave out a nervous laugh.

Reinaldo looked puzzled as all eyes turned to him.

He hadn't done anything wrong that he could remember. No one could have complained about him taking some old weeds from the empty lot, could they?

Derrick, who was glad someone else was in the hot seat for a change, whispered, "Ooooo, you're in big trouble now, Reinaldo."

Reinaldo still looked puzzled as Mrs. Levine continued. "Oh, you had to take Maria to the doctor this morning for a bad rash. That's too bad." Mrs. Levine held the phone away, and the class could hear a loud stream of words in Spanish. With her free hand, Mrs. Levine was motioning to Reinaldo to come up and interpret what his mother was saying.

Reinaldo, however, was not looking at Mrs. Levine. As soon as he heard the word rash, he had started unbuttoning his cuffs and rolling up his shirtsleeves. Sure enough, both arms were covered with red, oozing skin. No wonder he had been so uncomfortable all morning.

That's when the room erupted into chaos.

"Gross!"

"That's nasty!"

"Get away from me!"

These shouts came from the students sitting closest to Reinaldo. The students in the back of the room were clamoring out of their seats to look at Reinaldo and see what the fuss was about. Mrs. Santiago could still be heard above the other noise, yelling something in Spanish that no one understood. Mrs. Levine was still trying to get Reinaldo to take the phone.

Finally Mrs. Santiago spoke two words in English,

and all at once Mrs. Levine understood the whole situation. The words were POISON IVY. She realized that Reinaldo must have chosen poison ivy leaves for his sun print, given them to his sister to play with, and both of them had broken out in rashes as a result. Now that she understood the problem, Mrs. Levine quickly took charge again.

"Back to your seats, everyone!" she commanded as she picked up the dangling phone receiver and tried to calm down Mrs. Santiago.

"I'm sorry, Mrs. Santiago. With your permission I'll bring Reinaldo home myself while the other students are having lunch. I'm sorry, Mrs. Santiago. I didn't think poison ivy grew in the city, especially at this time of year. I'm sorry, Mrs. Santiago…"

No one in the class said a word when they finally saw Mrs. Levine hang up the phone and reach for her bottle of Tylenol.

Chapter 6

The remainder of the week passed quickly, and every day several more students brought in their leaf sun prints. Every bit of free time was spent looking up leaves in the reference books. Jazmin and Tonya even stayed after school to work on the project. Reinaldo came back to school on Wednesday. He was covered with calamine lotion but was not contagious.

Friday morning went by in a flurry of activity as the students were putting down their final guesses for the contest.

"Has anyone discovered the names of all of the leaves?" Mrs. Levine asked just before lunchtime. No one raised his or her hand. Most of the students still had three or four that they couldn't get, and no one had identified Janie's leaves. Her leaves were shaped like little bow ties centered exactly on the stem. Even Mrs. Levine admitted that she was stumped.

"I don't think that having more time will help. Hand me your papers, and after lunch we'll reveal the answers."

The cafeteria food was gulped down in record time

that day. All of the students were anxious to get back to the classroom to find out the results of the contest. Even the green beans that accompanied the grilled cheese sandwich were swallowed quickly. Nobody wanted to waste time today arguing with Mrs. Smith, the lunchroom lady.

Mrs. Smith looked like everyone's grandma, with her brown skin creased with wrinkles and her thin gray hair pulled back in a bun. She wore thick knee-high stockings, sensible shoes, and a white apron that was barely big enough to fit around her ample waist.

"Grandma Smith," as the kids called her, was a no nonsense kind of person. The only thing she disliked more than rude children was wasted food. No child was allowed outside for recess until all of his vegetables were eaten. Of course, her job was much harder on rainy days when students had been known to dawdle twenty minutes over one string bean. Grandma Smith came with built-in radar. She could spot a child slipping a stalk of broccoli into his pocket three tables away.

"We'll start with Derrick, and each person in order will take his leaf out of the envelope and identify it for us," said Mrs. Levine as soon as they all were back in the classroom. "Speak clearly and loudly so we can all hear you."

"I have a grape leaf, or *Vitis labrusca* as they say in Rome. And the grapes were good too," said Derrick. Everyone laughed except Mrs. Levine, who was secretly thanking God that Derrick had not gotten sick eating too many grapes. She'd dealt with enough angry parents over this project.

Around the room they went. Brandon revealed his sugar maple, *Acer saccharum*, leaf, Debra, her chestnut oak, *Quercus prinus*, Jazmin, her golden weeping willow, *Salix alba tristis*.

When they got to Reinaldo, Mrs. Levine said, "I hope you don't have your poison ivy, *Rhus radicans*, leaf with you. Your rash is proof enough of your leaf's identity. I assume everyone in the class got that one right." Reinaldo grinned sheepishly while the rest of the class laughed.

They continued on around the room until only Jeanetta and Janie were left. Jeanetta took out an orchid leaf from her mother's collection of Hawaiian orchids. Several students identified it correctly, because they knew that Jeanetta's mom raised orchids. They proved it when they found its picture in Mrs. Levine's book of exotic plants.

Then it was Janie's turn. "Instead of bringing just a leaf to show you, I brought the whole tree," said Janie, reaching under her desk for the big cardboard box she had put there that morning.

"You can't fit no tree in a box," Derrick said.

Even Mrs. Levine had a skeptical look on her face as Janie carefully took the cover off the box. She reached in and pulled out the weirdest tree anyone had ever seen. The bottom was a paper cup filled with plaster. Stuck in the plaster was a branch from a maple tree, but the leaves were definitely not maple leaves. This was a colorful tree with fan-folded leaves that had been pinched in the center to look like bow ties.

"What is this?" said Mrs. Levine while coming closer to get a better look.

"This is the money tree, or *Arbor pecunia*, that my Dad got for his thirtieth birthday. The guys at the firehouse gave it to him so that he could buy his big screen TV. Of course my father spent all of the real money, so I had to make new leaves out of monopoly money—just like a real deciduous tree that loses its leaves in the fall and gets new ones in the spring. Right, Mrs. Levine?"

Mrs. Levine didn't answer right away. She was too busy examining the pink, blue, and gold leaves that were really $5, $50, and $500 Monopoly bills when you looked closely. "Well, it certainly is colorful," said Mrs. Levine noncommittally.

"Awwww, Miz Levine that ain't no real tree," complained Derrick.

"Yeah," chimed in all of the other boys.

"But you said it didn't have to be an outdoor tree," said Janie. "And you didn't say it had to be a real tree."

"Yeah," added all of the other girls.

Mrs. Levine thought for a minute more and then spoke. "I've decided to accept this, Janie. You obviously spent a lot of time on this project and even looked up a Latin name. Congratulations! Because of your creativity you have won the prize for the most unusual leaf." As she was saying this, Mrs. Levine was making a mental note to be more explicit in giving directions next time. More than twenty years of teaching, she thought, and her students still surprised her.

When the contest entries were corrected, it was

determined that Jeanetta had the most correct answers. This didn't surprise anyone. The other kids had long ago gotten used to the idea that Jeanetta Jones was the best at everything, but because she didn't lord it over them, nobody stayed mad at her for long. Janie and Jeanetta couldn't wait to use their prizes, which were gift certificates to Pizza Hut. They were already planning a joint trip with their parents.

The girls also each received a book about nature. Jeanetta put hers in her bedroom. She could barely squeeze it into the pine bookcase that already had sagging shelves from the weight of all the books. Janie's book would end up under her bed with the dust bunnies, the dirty socks, and the remains of last year's Easter basket.

Mrs. Levine, who was quick to take advantage of any teaching opportunity that presented itself, set the class to work figuring out how much money there was altogether on Janie's money tree. Various students around the room could be heard muttering things like, "Thanks a lot, Janie!" and "We'll get you for this, Janie."

Lamar spoke for the rest of the class when he said, "My mother always told me money didn't grow on trees. I guess she was wrong."

Chapter 7

The next few weeks flew by as the students learned more and more about George Eastman and photography. They had fun making their own dark chamber (*camera obscura*) to replicate the ones used in France in the 1800s. Mrs. Smith donated the box that her new lunchroom freezer came in. With sides that measured six feet by four feet by three feet, it was just the right size for one student to fit in when it was placed on end. The sides had to be carefully taped so that absolutely no light could get in.

Then the box had to be painted totally black inside and out. When Mrs. Levine said, "I do not want to waste any valuable learning time with painting," Reinaldo, Lamar, and Derrick volunteered to stay after school to do the work. The boys were anxious to prove to Mrs. Levine that they could do something right—well, almost right.

Mrs. Levine's policy was to avoid problems before they could happen if at all possible. She provided the boys with some of her husband's old shirts and baseball caps to protect their clothes and hair. She also had them put plastic bread wrappers over their feet and tie them at their ankles so that their parents couldn't complain about paint on their shoes. She brought an old sheet from home to set the box on while being painted and a small cardboard box to set the paint can into. It was an unusually warm autumn day, and she opened all the classroom windows so they wouldn't be overcome by paint fumes.

"There. I've thought of everything," she said as she started to correct spelling tests and the boys began to paint.

Lamar started painting on the inside as Reinaldo and Derrick worked on the outside. Mr. Rivera, the custodian, supervised while they cut a door into one side. Even the edges of the door had to be painted black and then taped up when someone was inside.

Everything would have been perfect if it hadn't been for that darned wasp.

The boys were finishing up and checking for missed spots when all of a sudden a hornet appeared inside the box with Lamar. Lamar, who was normally calm and unexciteable, panicked when he heard the buzz, buzz, buzzing around his ear. Once, twice, three times he swatted the wasp with his paintbrush, but that only made the stinging invader angrier. Still swinging the paintbrush, he leaped out of the box, tripped over the can of paint, and fell on his stomach. The paint was spilled, and Lamar landed half on and half off the sheet. By the time Mrs. Levine got there with the fly swatter, Reinaldo and Derrick were wildly flinging their paint-brushes at the hornet, which had given up on Lamar and was now chasing them.

Mrs. Levine killed the hornet with one loud thwack of the fly swatter and then slowly looked around to assess the damage. By this time, Lamar had managed to stand up again and also right the paint can, but the spilled paint left quite a large black spot in the middle of the classroom floor. This was surrounded by lots of black footprints made by Derrick and Reinaldo as they tried to avoid the angry hornet. Mrs. Levine sadly sank to the floor after letting out one of her famous sighs (nine on a scale of one to ten).

"Look, Mrs. Levine," said Lamar. "The black paint spilled into the shape of New York State. And one of the footprints looks like Long Island." He was desperately trying to find something good about the situation.

Mrs. Levine lifted one eyebrow and looked again at the black mess. With a glimmer of hope in her voice she said, "Maybe you're right, Lamar. Derrick, take those dirty bags off your feet and go ask Mr. Rivera if he will help us clean up this mess." By the time Derrick returned with Mr. Rivera, Mrs. Levine was already thinking of ways to turn the mistake on the floor into a lesson on the geography of New York State.

Sitting inside of a camera (the big black box) was spooky but fun. Only Debra absolutely refused to get into that small, dark space with only a pinhole of light and close the door. "You're not putting me in something that looks like a coffin," she said.

"But look at the pictures you can make," said Janie.

"I've got a great one here of Jeanetta."

The black box pinhole camera used no film. Instead, the light shining through the pinhole projected an image from outside the box onto a white piece of paper hanging inside the box. The person in the box "took the picture" by tracing the image onto the white paper. After all, the word photography means "writing with light." The only problem was that the image was upside down and reversed left to right. So when Janie traced Jeanetta's image it looked like she was standing on her head.

Mrs. Levine had explained that they were supposed to turn the pictures right side up when they were done, but the class liked the reverse images better. Soon the classroom was full of pictures of trees, flowers, street lamps, and people all upside down. They even scanned some of the pictures into the computer and sent them by e-mail to Miss Robinson at the Sunny Hill Nursing Home.

Over the summer Mrs. Levine had made a valiant effort to join the electronic age. "I can't let Miss Robinson's gift go to waste," Mrs. Levine said to her husband when she signed up for a computer class in July. That's where she learned how to scan pictures into the computer. She also learned about e-mail and even had her own screen name (meanlevine), but as far as she was concerned, nothing would replace writing an old-fashioned letter on flowery, pink stationery using a nice fountain pen.

Chapter 8

As the days went on, the students progressed from drawing pictures of images in a box to making pinhole cameras out of oatmeal boxes. The worst part of that project was that Mr. Levine had to eat all of the oatmeal. Even oatmeal cookies lost their appeal after awhile. He said that this was the worst project his wife had gotten him into since she did a unit on Australia. That time he had to drive all over New York State looking for ostrich eggs. But at least he hadn't had to eat any ostriches or their eggs.

The next step was to make a camera out of a roll of Kodacolor II C126 film and the box it came in. The box, which measured three by five by nine-and-a-half centimeters, became the camera, and the kids learned how to use a taped-up pencil to advance the film from one frame to the next. Reinaldo learned this the hard way when he got his pencil jammed in the camera on the first frame and couldn't get it out. The film didn't move, and all of his pictures were on top of each other. Everyone laughed except Mrs. Levine, who was trying to think of how she could explain this in Spanish to

Mrs. Santiago.

Finally they were ready for real cameras, real film, and a real trip to George Eastman House. Miss Robinson, their benefactor from the lighthouse, provided them each with a brand new Kodak Instamatic camera. The students had been e-mailing Miss Robinson every day with their new computers (she bought herself one, too). When she heard about their interest in photography, Miss Robinson insisted on buying the cameras as well.

"Why aren't we using digital cameras?" Tomas wanted to know.

"How do you know about digital cameras?" said Mrs. Levine.

"Because my uncle has one. It's a Ni…"

"We only use Kodak cameras here in Rochester," interrupted Mrs. Levine, "and I want you to learn about film. You can't learn about film from a digital camera. Besides, we have Ms. Jones, Jeanetta's mom, who works at Kodak and has arranged for us to get our pictures developed free. Ms. Jones has also arranged to take a day off so that she can accompany us on our trip. Aren't we lucky to have her?"

On Thursday, November 17, a swarm of human-sized bumblebees could be seen gathered in front of School #27 on the Central Park side. The yellow and black creatures were not bumblebees at all, but rather the students from Mrs. Levine's fifth grade class. Last year the class had decided to wear yellow T-shirts and black pants on all of their field trips. The T-shirts had their names on them, along with an emblem of a bumblebee to stand for Susan "Bee" Anthony School #27. Mrs. Levine and Ms. Jones were also wearing their school T-shirts and could be seen buzzing back and forth within the swarm.

"I can't imagine what happened to Ms. Green," said Mrs. Levine. "Are you sure you told your mother 9:00 A.M., Lamar? She's always so prompt."

Lamar's mother had agreed to be the other chaperone for their trip. Last year, Janie's dad and Derrick's mom had accompanied them on most of their field trips—mainly so they could make Janie and Derrick behave.

"Yes," said Lamar. "I heard her tell the boss on the phone that the trip was at 9:00 A.M., and that she would be in to work as soon as it was over. She said she'd never been to a mansion and wanted to see how the rich folks lived."

Just then a stereo on wheels came speeding down the street and screeched to a halt directly in front of #27 School and the assembled students. Lamar knew without turning to look that it could only be his brother Steven. Steven was nineteen and drove a black Mustang with a sound system that was louder than the whole Rochester Philharmonic Orchestra, including the percussion instruments. He worked nights at the Mini-Mart on Norton Street, slept while Lamar was at school, and then baby-sat him until their parents got home at 6:00 P.M.

Lamar ran over to the car and shouted to be heard above the noise. "WHERE'S MAMA? SHE WAS S'POSED TO BE HERE AT NINE O'CLOCK."

Steven turned off the car and started to explain.

"Mama got a call from Aunt Doris just as she was fixing to leave for the school. Uncle Henry had one of his spells, and she didn't know what to do. Mama got me up and had me drive her over to Aunt Doris' place. She told me to get over here to take her place on the trip. She said it wouldn't hurt me to see how those rich folks lived."

With his shirt sticking out, his pants falling down, and his shoes untied, Steven looked like he had just fallen out of bed and gotten dressed in thirty seconds. In other words, he looked like almost every other teenage boy in Rochester. It didn't matter what time of the day it was. A gray hooded sweatshirt with huge pockets completed Steven's outfit. Something told Mrs. Levine not to even ask if he would trade it for a yellow #27 School T-shirt. "We're glad to have you, Steven," said Mrs. Levine, trying to make the most of a bad situation. Steven, who was one of Mrs. Levine's former students, was not her idea of an ideal chaperone, but he was another body and all that was available at the moment. "While you pull your car into the school parking lot, I'll make you a nametag, and then we'll get started walking to the Eastman House."

"Nametag? Walking?" said Steven, looking at Mrs. Levine like she was speaking a foreign language. "Mama didn't say nothin' about walkin'." Steven hadn't walked anywhere since he bought his car a year ago.

"Why, yes," replied Mrs. Levine. "Don't you remember from being in my class, Steven, that we always wear nametags wherever we go, and we walk whenever we can? It saves money and it's good exercise, too.

Exercise the body and you also exercise the mind, I always say."

With those words, Mrs. Levine took off down Central Park, motioning everyone to follow her. Ms. Jones fell in place in the middle of the group, and Steven brought up the rear. Steven, at six feet three inches tall, stood out in a crowd. Looking back, Mrs. Levine could easily see his gray hood towering at least a foot above her students. This was in spite of the fact that Steven did his best to slouch into the sidewalk. He was secretly praying that none of his friends would come by and see him.

Maybe this will work out after all, thought Mrs. Levine. If only she had known what lay ahead…

Chapter 9

"What do you think she'll make us learn today?" whispered Derrick to Lamar as they walked down Central Park. He knew that Mrs. Levine could not resist the urge to teach them something as they marched along.

Before Lamar could reply, Mrs. Levine turned to face the group and said, "Let's practice our multiplication facts while we're walking. I just happen to have the multiplication rap tape and my pocketsize player with me. Steven, we know you like rap music. Join in when you catch on. Steven's reply was just a roll of the eyes, but Mrs. Levine appeared not to notice as she started in on two times one equals two.

In no time at all, they had turned the corner onto North Goodman, crossed over Main Street, zigzagged over to South Goodman, and turned left onto East Avenue. By the time they were rapping nine times seven equals sixty-three, they found themselves in sight of the ninety-three year old mansion. Although school groups were supposed to enter Eastman House from the museum in the rear, Mrs. Levine wanted her kids to enter through the front door like Mr. Eastman's

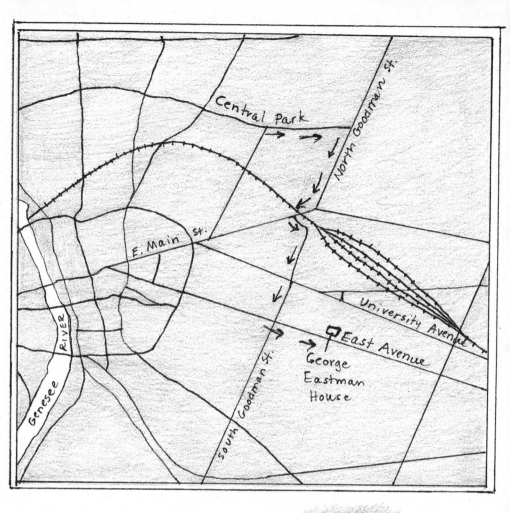

distinguished guests.

"Oh, there it is," shouted Janie. "It's got those tall things like in the picture."

Mrs. Levine and Ms. Jones laughed. Steven was gawking at the mansion like the younger kids. "Those tall things are pillars, Janie. Don't they look majestic?" said Mrs. Levine.

"What's that green stuff growing on the outside?" asked Reinaldo. "That's not poison ivy, is it? My mother will kill me if I get poison ivy again."

"She'll kill me too," said Mrs. Levine under her breath.

"Don't worry, Reinaldo," said Ms. Jones. "It's ivy alright, but it's English ivy and not poison ivy. It has tiny feet that grab onto spaces between the bricks. English ivy loves houses like this."

"Why does it have so many chimneys?" asked Lamar.

"Hey, bro, a house like this needs more than one fireplace. Even I know that," answered Steven. Mrs. Levine just nodded in agreement.

All of a sudden Reinaldo took a step backward. "Does this place have a ghost like the lighthouse did?" he said. He looked ready to run at the first sign of trouble.

"No, I've never heard of a ghost living here," answered Mrs. Levine. "Besides, I don't believe in ghosts. Ms. Jones, Mr. Green, and I will now pass out the cameras. Make sure you get the one with your name on it."

It took a full minute for Steven to realize that Mrs. Levine was talking about him when she said Mr. Green. But then he slouched forward and helped get the children equipped with their cameras. Steven already knew most of the kids from the neighborhood. In fact, last year he had taken his brother Lamar and friends Derrick and Reinaldo on their unsuccessful trip to the beach to look for buried treasure. The ones he didn't know already, he could pick out by reading their names on their T-shirts.

In no time at all, every student was armed with his or her camera securely strapped around the neck. Mrs. Levine had wisely used some of Miss Robinson's money to purchase camera straps. "Cameras are too expensive to drop and break," she said.

At the sound of twenty-four cameras all clicking at once, Mrs. Levine stepped forward again. "Remember not to waste your film. Take a few pictures of the front of the house, and when we get inside look for things related to plants and animals. I have a prize for the person who can take the most interesting plant and animal pictures."

"Sure," whispered Janie to Jeanetta. "The prize is probably another science book."

Jeanetta had no time to reply, for at that moment the double doors swung wide open, and a short lady with gray hair and big round eyeglasses with red frames stepped out to greet them.

"Welcome to George Eastman House. I'm Ms. Hamilton, your docent." Ms. Hamilton wore a gray flannel suit with a gray blouse and red high-heeled shoes. It didn't seem possible that such a small lady could have such a deep, booming voice.

"Are you George Eastman's mother?" said Tomas.

"Can we take your picture?" said Justina.

"What's a dokin?" said Debra, mispronouncing the new word.

Ms. Hamilton let out one long, loud laugh and said, "Step inside and I will answer all of your questions."

No one said a word. In fact, no one took a breath as they stepped over the threshold of 900 East Avenue into the huge entrance hall with the white marble floor. The floor was so shiny that they could almost see themselves in it. Straight ahead was the biggest staircase that most of them had ever seen. All of the braver children in the class were eyeing the curved mahogany railing with longing.

"Move over here and I'll show you the living room first," said Ms. Hamilton as she stepped out of the way to allow a group of middle-aged ladies in purple blazers to pass by. "The museum is so crowded today. That group is the Flower City Lilac Society. The people in white blazers are the Episcopal Church Women. There are also other school groups here."

"Now, to answer your questions, a docent is a fancy name for teacher. I'll be your docent for the next hour, but I don't like to have my picture taken. No, I am not George Eastman's mother. George and his mother Maria both died many years ago, but if you look behind me you can see a big picture of Mother on the wall."

"What about Mr. Eastman's wife and kids?" asked Lamar.

"Mr. Eastman never married and had no children."

"You mean he lived in this huge house all alone?

"All alone with Mother and the servants. Actually

Mr. Eastman had lots of company here. He always had some out of town visitor sleeping in one of his fifteen bedrooms, and he was famous for his Sunday night suppers. He would invite one hundred people every week to hear music and share a meal. He often gave the ladies an orchid from his greenhouse. Besides photography, Mr. Eastman loved flowers and music."

"Mom, I bet you would have liked Mr. Eastman's orchids," Jeanetta said.

"Fifteen bedrooms and no kids," said Derrick. "That's not fair! I have to share my bedroom with Louis and Richard."

Ms. Hamilton continued. "The Sunday night musicales were held in this very room. Look at the corners of the ceiling before we move on. You will see a plaque in each corner showing one of the four seasons. See if you can tell which one is autumn. Then lets move on to the conservatory."

"What's a conservatory?" said several students all at once. They had squeezed past a group of students from #22 School and entered a big, open room with walls of windows and an organ and lots of plants.

"It's just what you see," answered Ms. Hamilton. "A conservatory is a place for plants or music or both." No one was listening to her anymore, though, because all eyes were riveted on the huge gray elephant head mounted on the wall.

"Wow!" Click.

"Awesome!" Click.

"Is it real?" Click.

"Where's the rest of the elephant?" Click.

Everyone started talking and snapping pictures at the same time.

"George Eastman had another hobby besides photography. He liked to go on safaris to Africa and shoot large game animals with a rifle," explained Ms. Hamilton. "Today we only shoot these animals with our cameras. The elephant you see here is just a replica of the original one that used to hang here. But the tusk you see on the floor is a real ivory tusk. Come with me to the billiard room, and I will show you some evidence of the other animals that Mr. Eastman collected."

"I feel like I'm in the middle of a game of Clue," whispered Jamie to Jeanetta. "Next thing you know we'll be taking the secret passage to the kitchen."

"Or maybe you'll both get knocked on the head by the candlestick," threatened Derrick, who had overheard Jamie's remarks. Little did they know just how important a candlestick would become.

Chapter 10

Reluctantly, Mrs. Levine's class left the conservatory, but not before everyone had taken at least one more picture of the elephant head.

"Excuse us, excuse us," called out Ms. Hamilton as they brushed by another group of school children. When they entered the billiard room they could see the purple blazers of the Flower City Lilac Society exiting through the other door.

"Oh, there's my friend Mrs. Whitman," said Mrs. Levine. "Hello, Lois," she called out. Lois was one of the ladies in purple blazers and was hurrying to catch up with the rest of the group.

Although the room was dominated by a big billiard table, that was not what most of the kids noticed first as they slowly filled up the room.

"Look! I see butterflies on the floor," yelled out Janie as many of the other students looked down and started snapping pictures. The butterflies were not real. They were actually small pieces of dark teak wood that were being used to fit together the light teak wood planks that made up the billiard room floor.

Lamar was not looking at the butterflies on the floor. His eyes were drawn to the sofa, where a blanket made up of raccoon skins was thrown over the back. Lamar thought the patterns in the raccoon fur were cool, but all he could picture was a bunch of raccoons running around naked.

Reinaldo's eyes found an ashtray that was like no ashtray he had ever seen. A metal dish for the ashes was set on top of an animal's foot. He thought the foot must have belonged to a bull or a moose or maybe even Paul Bunyon's big blue ox, Babe. He cautiously got in close to take a picture, all the while imagining being trampled by this big beast.

Derrick didn't notice the room's furnishings at all. He was staring at the stern-faced man who was dressed in blue and was standing in the corner. "Who called the police?" he cried out, while wondering in his head if he had done anything lately that would interest the police. Maybe they had heard that he had broken Mrs. Blackwood's fence when he decided to take a shortcut to school last week. Derrick was always feeling guilty about something.

"I'm not the police," spoke up the tall man, who was now smiling. "I'm a Peerless detective, and I'm here to prevent a crime. Some of the things in this house are very expensive and cannot be replaced. It's my job to see to it that nothing gets lost or stolen."

Even Steven seemed to be impressed by this room and its contents. He was thinking how cool it would be to have a room like this where he and the boys could hang out. All it needed was a CD player and a couple of speakers. He pictured himself with a cue stick in one hand, a cigar in the other, sinking the eight ball in the corner pocket while the guys said things like, "How'd you do that?" Steven's daydream was interrupted by Ms. Hamilton. She instructed them to move on to the library so that the Episcopal ladies could move into their spot.

The library had floor to ceiling books on every wall, but only Jeanetta seemed impressed. She had never seen so many books in one house before, and she could easily imagine spending the rest of the day curled up with a mystery story in some quiet corner of this beautiful house. "I don't see any animals in here to take pictures of," said Derrick.

"Well, there aren't any actual animals in here, Derrick, but the top of this desk is made from a rhinoceros' hide," explained Ms. Hamilton. They all spent the next few minutes touching and taking pictures of the unusual desk.

"I never thought I'd pet a rhinoceros," said Janie as she posed for Jeanetta's camera.

Derrick pointed at Janie and said, "Look, a rhinoceros and a pi...." An icy glare from Mrs. Levine prevented him from finishing that sentence.

From the library they went back to the front hall and up the beautiful stairs to the second floor. These rooms were not kept as bedrooms, but held museum displays. There was only one room that was fun. In that room they could touch everything. They used stereoscopes

and made their own thaumatropes. They learned that the thaumatrope was named after its inventor and is a scientific device used to show the principle of persistence of vision. It consists of a round disc with a different picture on each side. When the disc is spun, the two pictures merge into one because an image of the first picture stays on your retina while you look at the second. Jeanetta drew one of a dog and a bone. Derrick drew one of a kid and a bike.

Finally their time was up, and Mrs. Levine promised them a trip back to learn how to develop film. It was just as they were coming back down the grand staircase that all the commotion started.

Chapter 11

The front hall was swarming with people as Mrs. Levine's class descended the stairs. The ladies in purple blazers were going from the living room to the conservatory. The white blazers were moving from the library to the living room. The St. Stanislaus students were walking from the billiard room to the library, and the #22 School students were heading up the stairs. Ms. Hamilton deftly led her charges through the mob and into the dining room. She had just started explaining how George Eastman had put his initials on all of his china, crystal, silver, and dining room linens, when there came a loud shriek from the conservatory.

"Help! Help! Mildred has fainted. Stand back and give her room to breathe," shouted one of the purple blazers as she bent over her friend.

Mr. Greeley, the Peerless detective, rushed by Mrs. Levine's group and quickly attended to the lady on the floor. "Let me help you up," he said to the dazed woman who had just regained consciousness. "Someone get her some water. I think she fainted just because it's so hot in here and there are so many people."

"I feel so embarrassed," said Mildred as she sank into the chair that Detective Greeley was holding for her.

"No need to be embarrassed, ma'am. It happens all the time when the museum gets crowded. I guess they overbooked for today. Now that you're all right, everyone can go back to their tours."

Mrs. Levine's class reassembled in the dining room, and Ms. Hamilton quickly finished her talk about all of the meals served there. She ended the tour of the dining room by letting everyone peer over the rope into the safe where all of the expensive dishes and silver were kept.

"Is there any money in there?" asked Derrick. He just couldn't imagine a safe, especially a room-sized one, without any money in it.

"No, Derrick, I'm sorry to disappoint you, but Mr. Eastman kept all of his money in the bank," explained Ms. Hamilton. "This safe held all of his unusual and expensive pieces of porcelain and silver. He was not worried so much about burglars as he was about dishonest servants stealing from him. Look at how thick the safe door is. It would be awfully hard to break into."

"Finish taking your pictures here, boys and girls," instructed Mrs. Levine. "We'll be leaving soon, and I'll be collecting the cameras for the walk home."

After thank-yous and good-byes, Ms. Hamilton escorted the tired children slowly down the back hall. They had entered through the front door, but were leaving by the back door. "I wonder if this was how the servants felt," said Janie as she got in line with the rest of the group and began to file out.

Chapter 12

All but three of the students were out the back door when they heard a loud voice from inside yelling, "Stop! Stop! Don't let anyone leave." It was Detective Greeley, running down the back hall shouting to the guard at the door. "One of the silver candlesticks is missing, and we can't let anyone leave here until we've searched for it."

Just at that moment there was a loud CLANG, and everyone turned to see a silver candlestick rolling around on the sidewalk. The sapphires that were embedded in the base of the candlestick were giving off sparks of light as the sun reflected off them.

"It fell out of that young man's sweatshirt pocket," announced Detective Greeley. He was pointing at Steven. "Did anyone else see it fall? What about you two boys?" he asked, looking at Derrick and Lamar. They had been standing right near Steven. Derrick looked at Lamar. Lamar looked at Derrick. Then they both looked at the ground.

"Well, er, ah, I'm not sure what I saw," mumbled Derrick.

"Me either," added Lamar.

"Let me help," spoke up Ms. Levine. "Derrick and Lamar, you must speak the truth so that we can get to the bottom of this matter."

Neither boy could lie outright to his teacher. "I guess the candlestick fell out of Steven's pocket," said Derrick.

"Yeah, I guess it did," said Lamar.

"There must be no guessing about it," said their teacher firmly. "Either you saw the candlestick fall from Steven's pocket or you didn't."

"I saw it fall," said Derrick in a very soft voice.

"I did too," said Lamar even more softly. His eyes were still on the ground. He just couldn't bear to look at his older brother.

All this time, Steven just stood there with his mouth open, saying nothing. He had been more surprised than anyone else to see the candlestick fall out of his pocket, and he bent down now to pick it up.

"Don't touch that candlestick!" cautioned Mrs. Levine. She had learned something from being married to a lawyer for twenty-three years.

Detective Greeley pulled a handkerchief out of his back pocket and retrieved the candlestick from where it had come to rest against an outside wall.

"Why did you try to steal that candlestick, son?" said Detective Greeley, turning his attention once again to Steven.

"I didn't try to steal no candlestick," said Steven.

"Then why did you have it in your pocket?"

"I didn't know it was in my pocket 'til it fell out.

Honest!"

"I'd like to believe that, Steven, but that candlestick must weigh at least three pounds. How could you not know it was in your pocket?"

"I felt something pulling on my pocket, but I thought it was just Lamar and Derrick messing with me," explained Steven. "I thought if I didn't pay them no mind, they'd stop it. I didn't try to steal nothing, honest!"

A large crowd had begun to gather now, everyone stretching their necks and leaning forward to hear what was going on.

"That teenager tried to steal the candlestick."

"That teenager tried to steal the candlestick."

"That teenager tried to steal the candlestick."

These words were passed on and on to each interested newcomer like the water bucket in the old time fire brigade.

Steven was cursing his mother for getting him involved in this mess to begin with. It wasn't his idea to go on this trip.

Lamar just wanted to melt into the sidewalk.

The rest of the class wasn't sure what to think. No one wanted to believe Steven was guilty, but the candlestick had come out of Steven's pocket.

Mrs. Levine thought that this was probably the worst day in all of her years of teaching. After letting out the biggest sigh of her career (fifteen on a scale of one to ten), she strode up to Detective Greeley and said, "I know this young man is innocent. If you will let me use your phone I'll call my husband. He's a lawyer, and he will come right over to help settle this. Meanwhile the children, Ms. Jones, and I must begin walking back to school."

After using the phone she turned to Steven and said, "I believe you are innocent, Steven. You might not have been the best student I ever had, but I always thought you were trustworthy. Mr. Levine will be right over to help you out. Then he'll take you back to get your car and go home with you to talk to your parents."

Steven didn't answer. He just nodded his head. He couldn't believe that he had forgotten about his car. If only he had just kept on driving this morning right on by the school, or better yet, just stayed in bed.

Chapter 13

It was a very subdued group of children who lined up on the sidewalk for the walk back to school. But as soon as they were off Eastman House property and onto University Avenue, everyone seemed to talk at once.

"Will Steven have to go to jail?"

"Will we ever see him again?"

"Are they going to kill him?"

"My cousin got killed in jail."

"Can I have Steven's car?"

These were only some of the questions that stopped Mrs. Levine in her tracks.

"I was going to wait until we got back to school to discuss this, but maybe we'd better stop for a minute and talk about it right now," she said. "Everyone sit for a minute right here on the sidewalk."

When everyone looked somewhat comfortable, she began. "Mr. Levine will come and talk with Steven and Detective Greeley to see if they can figure out exactly what happened. Then Mr. Levine will bring Steven home, and he will be able to go to work and sleep in his own bed tonight. The director of Eastman House will have to decide whether or not to press charges against Steven. Because the candlestick has been returned, they might just forget the whole thing.

"But, if they still think that Steven took the candlestick, then he will have to go to court. The judge or jury will then decide if he is guilty or innocent. If Steven is guilty, then he will have some kind of punishment. He probably will have to pay a fine or do some community service work. He probably won't go to jail. Meanwhile Steven will be able to work and drive his car just like he always does. He just won't be able to leave town. Does that answer all of your questions?"

Ms. Jones, Jeanetta's mother, had stayed in the background on this trip. She now spoke up. "Mrs. Levine, I don't have a question, but I agree with you. I know Steven and his parents, and I'm sure that he is innocent. Boys and girls, while we're walking the rest of the way home, I'd like you to search your minds and see if you can remember seeing anything unusual at Eastman House today. If Steven says he didn't put that candlestick in his pocket, then someone else did. It wasn't one of you playing a trick on Steven was it?" Both Mrs. Levine and Ms. Jones examined the students one by one to look for signs of guilt or deceit.

When they were satisfied that none of the students was involved, Mrs. Levine continued. "Ms. Jones, you have come up with an excellent idea. I should have thought of that myself. It looks like we have a mystery to solve. Please children, try hard to remember anything unusual at all. You never know what little piece of information might help Steven. It may be up to us to prove his innocence. If someone else put that candlestick in Steven's pocket, maybe one of us can figure out who it was."

"What makes that candlestick so special anyway?" asked Derrick.

"I heard someone say that the candlestick was a gift from King George V of England to George Eastman when he went to London to open one of his dental clinics," said Ms. Jones.

"Was George Eastman a dentist too?" Derrick said.

"No, Derrick. Mr. Eastman was not a dentist. He just earned lots of money from making cameras and film, and he liked to give his money away, so he paid for the dental clinic. He didn't work there."

"He gave his money away?" Derrick said in disbelief.

With that last comment, Mrs. Levine motioned the group to stand and follow her. The rest of the walk home was made in complete silence. Everyone was searching his or her memory for a way to help Steven.

Chapter 14

The next morning it was hard to get back to regular schoolwork after the excitement of the previous day. Mrs. Levine promised the class time later in the afternoon to brainstorm ideas about Steven and the candlestick.

Meanwhile everyone was being especially nice to Lamar. It was not hard to be nice to Lamar, because he was everybody's friend. But today the kids were treating him extra nicely. Derrick slipped a pack of gum into Lamar's desk as he passed by. Janie gave him her cookie at lunchtime. Reinaldo let him play with his electronic Battleship game at recess. Jeanetta wrote him a note but then was too embarrassed to give it to him. What if Lamar found out that she didn't just "like" him but that she "like liked" him? She tore up the note but slipped him a piece of her favorite red licorice.

Somehow they managed to get through reading one whole story in the reading book, five pages of language arts (paragraphs and main ideas), and one health worksheet before lunch. Then it was on to long division and science. At 2:00 P.M. Mrs. Levine stood up and said, "Let's clear off our desks and talk about what we've all been thinking about all day."

Janie wondered, as she always did, why Mrs. Levine didn't clean off her own desk when she said, "let's clear off our desks," but she decided against mentioning it.

"Now," began Mrs. Levine, "we have a mystery to solve, and when detectives in books try to solve a mystery, they often begin by making a list of things they know and things they don't know."

She strode to the chalkboard, made a line down the middle, and labeled the left side FACTS and the right side QUESTIONS. "The things we know are facts. The things we don't know are questions." In spite of the topic, Mrs. Levine smiled inside. She was thinking, "I just love it when I can turn a real situation into a classroom lesson."

"Now is the time to brainstorm. Close your eyes and picture us at the Eastman House. What do you see?"

"I see all those ladies in the purple coats," said Janie. "Purple's my favorite color, and I loved those blazers."

"Aw, what do the ladies in the purple coats have to do with Steven and the candlestick?" complained Derrick.

"It may not have anything to do with Steven," said Mrs. Levine, "but then again, maybe it does. That's what brainstorming is all about. You write down anything that comes into your mind. You never know what will be important. Continue, Janie."

As Mrs. Levine turned back to the blackboard, Janie stuck her tongue out at Derrick and continued. "Well, besides the ladies in the purple blazers, there were the ladies in the white blazers and all those kids from all those other schools."

"Let's just write that the Eastman House was very crowded yesterday," said Mrs. Levine, "and that there were many colorful things to look at. What else?"

"That lady fainted," said Debra.

"Yeah, and that policema…I mean detective went over to help her," added Derrick.

"What room was that in?" asked Mrs. Levine. So much had happened so fast that she wasn't sure herself.

"The lady fainted in the conservatory," said Reinaldo. "I remember her sitting under the elephant head. But I don't remember where Detective Greeley came from. He was just there all of a sudden."

"Don't you remember?" said Lamar. "He had been in the billiard room and then the dining room with us."

"We'll write that a lady—in a purple blazer, Janie— fainted in the conservatory and that Detective Greeley left the dining room to help her. Try now to think when the first time you saw that candlestick was."

"I didn't see it 'til it fell out of Steven's pocket," said Lamar quietly.

Jeanetta thought her heart would break to see Lamar looking so sad.

"I didn't see it either, Lamar," said Mrs. Levine, "but maybe somebody else did."

"I saw it before that," said Bobby. "It was sitting on top of that long, wooden piece of furniture along the wall in the dining room. There was a mirror behind it, and at first I thought it was part of a sword."

"Why would anyone have a sword in their dining

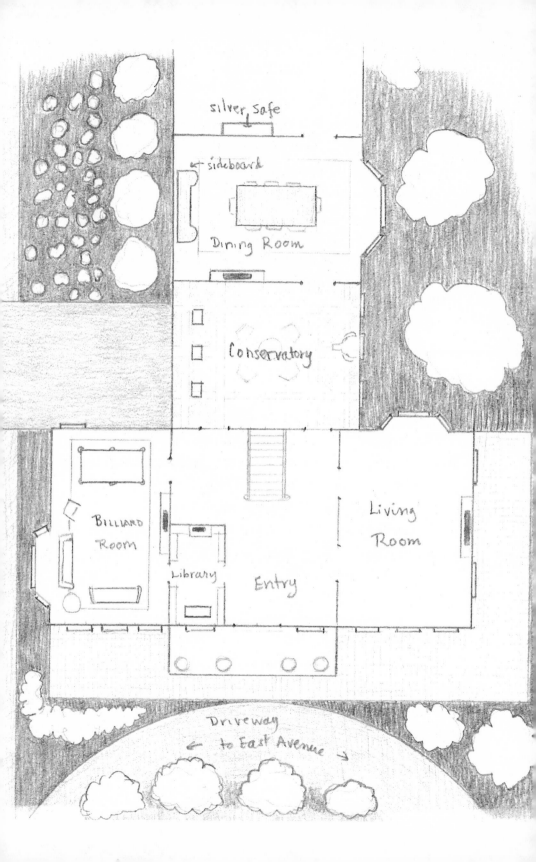

room?" said Derrick.

"To carve the roast elephant?" replied Bobby. Everyone laughed.

"Well, if anyone would have a sword in their dining room, I suppose it would be Mr. Eastman," said Mrs. Levine. "I'll write that the candlestick was on the sideboard in the dining room in front of the mirror. Think hard. Did any of you see somebody pick it up?"

"I saw one of the kids from #22 School touch it, but he didn't pick it up," said Shekeya.

"What if one of those other kids put it in Steven's pocket just to get him in trouble?" said Derrick.

"Why would they do that?" said Reinaldo.

"Just because."

"That's always a possibility, and we can't rule anything out so we'll put that on our question side of the board," said Mrs. Levine. She turned back to the board and wrote on the QUESTIONS side: Did another student take the candlestick and put it in Steven's pocket?

"Did anyone see the candlestick in Steven's pocket or hanging out of his pocket?" continued Mrs. Levine. When no one responded, she said, "I guess we'll have to write this on the question side of the board." She turned and added to the list: How did the candlestick get into Steven's pocket?

"Could the candlestick have just fallen into Steven's pocket?" said Janie.

"Good question, Janie," said Mrs. Levine. "It doesn't seem likely, but we can't rule out anything. Let's try a little experiment. Who has on a sweatshirt with big pockets?"

Several students raised their hands, and Mrs. Levine chose Reinaldo to come forward. "Okay, Reinaldo, we're going to pretend that you're Steven."

"Now what can we use for a candlestick?" she wondered aloud. "We need something not too tall and thin, but something that weighs a lot."

"That's Janie," called out Derrick.

"Ha, ha, very funny," said Janie. "How about your stapler, Mrs. Levine?" She was thinking that she'd like it to accidentally fall on Derrick's head.

"Great idea, Janie. You're really thinking today." Mrs. Levine grabbed the stapler off of her desk and stood next to Reinaldo.

"Reinaldo, you stand still. I'll hold the stapler up and drop it. Let's see if I can get it into your pocket."

After several unsuccessful attempts, Derrick said, "That's not fair, Miz Levine. Reinaldo has his arms covering the pockets. Make him move his arms forward or back."

So Reinaldo moved his arms forward. He moved his arms backward. He put his arms over his head. He bent over. But the results were the same. The stapler didn't come close to falling into Reinaldo's pocket.

Finally Mrs. Levine said, "I think we can safely conclude that the candlestick did not get into Steven's pocket accidentally. We can also conclude that I might need a new stapler after dropping this one so many times. Omigosh! Look at the time. Dismissal is in one minute. We'll have to continue with this tomorrow."

Chapter 15

By the next morning, one whole wall of Room 217 at Susan B. Anthony School was taken up with a FACTS/QUESTIONS chart. Mrs. Levine had spent time after school copying their list from the chalkboard onto chart paper. She was just admiring her work when Mr. Coley, the school principal, showed up at her door, and he was not alone. Behind him stood Lamar and Derrick and Reinaldo.

"What trouble did Derrick start now, Mr. Coley? Lamar, is that a band-aid above your eye?"

"I don't think it was Derrick who started the fight, Mrs. Levine," said Mr. Coley. Derrick smirked at his teacher, but didn't say a word. "From what I can gather, Tyrell Roberts from Mr. Bernard's class was calling Lamar's brother Steven a thief, among other things. Lamar got up to defend his brother, and one thing led to another. At some point Derrick and Reinaldo jumped into the fight, and Lamar cut his eye on the corner of a cafeteria table. We stopped at the nurse's office, and I had Ms. Jackson take a look at it before we came up here. She doesn't think he'll need stitches. I thought about sending all of them home, but I think the best thing is for them to stay in school and attend one of our new peer mediation sessions after school. Just keep an eye on that cut, Mrs. Levine." He looked at the boys. "You know that our school is supposed to be about learning how to get along without fighting."

"Tell that to Tyrell. He shouldn't be talkin' trash 'bout Lamar's brother."

"Derrick, we'll talk about it after school. And don't worry. Tyrell will be there too. Now go sit down and behave yourselves. I'm really disappointed in you, Lamar. You've never been in trouble before."

Mr. Coley gave them one last look, and Lamar wanted to melt into the floor again. Mrs. Levine let out one of her sighs (eight on a scale of one to ten) and sat down at her desk for a minute. Derrick was afraid they were going to get a lecture about not fighting, and he was mentally adding $100 to Mrs. Levine's bank account. At that moment the bell rang, and the other kids started filing in, all wanting to know what had happened to the boys. Mrs. Levine jumped up and steered everyone to their seats. When the last bell rang, she told the class what had happened and started in on the lecture that Derrick was expecting. When she was done, she drew everyone's attention to her new chart.

"Now. No more fight talk. Look over here, class. I put this FACTS and QUESTIONS chart up permanently so that we can be thinking about our mystery even while we're doing our other work today." (As if anybody was thinking about anything else.) "I'll try to save time at the end of every day to discuss this. Now take out your reading books."

Reading led into language arts, which led into spelling, and the day sped by. When it was discussion time, Derrick led off. "I've been thinking, Miz Levine. Besides knowing who put the candlestick in Steven's pocket, we need to know when it was done."

"I couldn't agree with you more, Derrick. In fact, knowing when the candlestick was moved may help us to figure out who moved it." She wrote on the QUESTIONS side of the chart: When was the candlestick put into Steven's pocket?

"Now, Bobby, did you or anyone else notice what time it was when you saw the candlestick in the dining room?"

Bobby and several others shook their heads no.

"Well, let's approach this a different way. We don't know the exact time, but we know the candlestick ended up in Steven's jacket sometime between when some of you saw it in the dining room and when it fell on the ground outside the door. How much time do you think it took for us to walk from the dining room to the back door?"

"Do you mean when we were in the dining room the first time or the second time?" said Jeanetta. "Remember we all rushed out of the dining room into the conservatory when that lady screamed and then went back into the dining room when we found out that she was all right."

"You're absolutely right, Jeanetta. I'd forgotten that we were in the dining room twice yesterday. Bobby, did you see the candlestick the first time we were in the dining room or the second time?"

"Gee, I know I saw it the first time we went into the

dining room, because that was the first thing I noticed. Like I said yesterday, I thought the candlestick might be part of a sword. I think it was there the second time, but I can't be sure. Maybe somebody else noticed it." The room got quiet as everyone waited for someone else to answer.

It turned out that no one could say for sure whether the candlestick was in the dining room the second time or not. Finally Mrs. Levine said, "We'll have to just conclude that the candlestick was moved some time between when we entered the dining room for the first time and when we tried to leave the museum. With all the commotion and the amount of people in the way, I'd say that had to have taken at least forty-five minutes. We were with the lady who fainted for at least ten minutes, and then we listened to the docent's description of the dining room. What was her name again?"

"Ms. Hamilton," Janie called out.

"That's right. Her name was Ms. Hamilton. I don't know where my mind is nowadays. Thank you, Janie. Anyway, all of that took time. Lamar, why don't you ask Steven when he first felt something tugging at his pocket? We'll continue this on Monday. Class, you may get ready for dismissal, and Derrick, Lamar, and Reinaldo, I'll walk you down to the peer mediation center. I wouldn't want you to get lost on the way."

Derrick gave Lamar a sympathetic punch in the arm and then turned around quickly to see if Mrs. Levine was watching. Luckily, she was busy telling Janie not to forget her math homework.

Chapter 16

"What about fingerprints, Mrs. Levine?" Reinaldo burst through the classroom door on Monday morning. "I saw a police show over the weekend, and they caught the bad guy 'cause his fingerprints were on the fireplace poker that he used to kill the rich guy."

"Hold that thought until our afternoon discussion time, Reinaldo. Ms. Jones has gotten our trip pictures back from being developed at Kodak, and I want you to look at those this morning."

If Reinaldo was the most enthusiastic person to enter the classroom that morning, then Lamar was the glummest. Mrs. Levine hoped that no one was bad-mouthing his brother again. Or maybe he had heard the same thing about Steven that she had heard. She made a mental note to talk to him about it later, but right now she couldn't wait to see the results of her class' first real picture-taking trip.

Ms. Jones passed out the pictures, and the class spent a half hour examining their own and their friends' pictures. Although Mrs. Levine had cautioned them to put their initials on the back of their own photographs,

Shakeya and Maria got in a fight over one of the elephant head pictures.

"I'll keep this myself," Mrs. Levine said angrily. "Now label your pictures before this happens again."

Soon Mrs. Levine began giving instructions for writing books about their experience. They were each to pick out a dozen of their best pictures, put them in sequence, and write about each one. "Remember to include sentences that tell about your feelings as well as descriptive sentences about what you saw. This is fifth grade, and I am expecting fifth grade work. No first grade sentences like: This is a table." Ms. Jones stayed to help and circulated around the room offering advice here and encouragement there. She helped Justina select which pictures to use for her book, and she helped Donald choose just the right word to describe a particular piece of furniture. She also got involved in the mystery and was on the lookout for any pictures of the candlestick or the dining room. No one could believe it when the lunch bell rang.

When discussion time came around, Mrs. Levine let Reinaldo lead off. "What about fingerprints?" asked Reinaldo. "Did the police check for fingerprints?"

"That's a great question, Reinaldo. I asked Mr. Levine the same thing. He said that the police found no fingerprints on the candlestick at all. That's not unusual because the museum people wear gloves when they handle the expensive silver so they will not tarnish it."

"But if Steven's fingerprints weren't on the candlestick, doesn't that mean that Steven couldn't have taken it?" insisted Reinaldo.

"Not necessarily," replied Mrs. Levine. "The police think that Steven covered his hand with his shirtsleeve when he picked up the candlestick or else wiped the prints clean with his sweatshirt before putting it in his pocket. I think that's preposterous! If Steven had actually taken the candlestick, he wouldn't have thought to erase his fingerprints. It was not a premeditated crime."

"What's a premeditated crime?" asked Justina

"That's a crime that's planned ahead of time," explained Mrs. Levine. "Even if Steven had taken the candlestick, he could not have planned it ahead since he didn't know until Tuesday morning that he was even going to be at the Eastman House."

"I still think he's innocent," said Reinaldo.

"Me, too."

"Me, too."

"Me, too." The rest of the class was quick to agree with Reinaldo.

"I agree," said Mrs. Levine. "We'll just have to work a little harder to prove it. Meanwhile I'll write on the FACTS side of our chart: There are no fingerprints on the candlestick."

"Doesn't that mean that a kid from one of the other schools probably didn't do it?" said Jeanetta. "I mean would a kid think to wipe his fingerprints off of the candlestick?"

"He would if he watched the same TV show I did," said Reinaldo.

"I see your point, Jeanetta," said Mrs. Levine. "If

another student is responsible for this, it would have been a spur of the moment impulse, as with Steven. We would expect to find his or her fingerprints on the candlestick. It sounds as if the real thief knew what he or she was doing. Although we can't be absolutely sure, I'd bet that an adult is responsible. If there is no more discussion about fingerprints I have something else to tell you." She paused and took a deep breath before opening her mouth again.

"Mr. Levine told me something else that I wasn't sure I should share with you, but it will come out in the newspaper anyway, and you need to know all of the facts in order to help solve the crime." She looked sadly at Lamar as she continued.

"Steven has been arrested once before for shoplifting, and that time he was guilty. Steven told Mr. Levine that he was fourteen years old at the time, and he stole a pack of cigarettes because he thought it would be cool. The clerk at the counter saw him do it and called the police. When the police learned about Steven's prior arrest, they became more determined than ever to find him guilty of the Eastman House crime.

"Steven said that when he saw his mother cry after that first arrest, he vowed that he would never steal again, and he says he hasn't. Mr. Levine and I believe in giving people second chances, and we think that Steven has kept his word and did not commit this crime. Like I've said before, I always thought Steven was trustworthy.

"I'm sorry that your family has had to go through this, Lamar. I still feel partly to blame for having Steven go with us in the first place. But this just means that we'll have to think harder and harder of a way to prove Steven innocent. Get those gray cells working, boys and girls, and we'll talk more tomorrow."

Chapter 17

On Tuesday morning Mrs. Levine allowed students who finished their reading and language arts assignments to look through the Eastman House photographs for clues of Steven's innocence. At 11:15 A.M. Janie let out an excited yell. "I think I found a clue!"

Work stopped as everyone looked at Janie.

"Tell us what you found," encouraged Mrs. Levine.

"I found this picture of the whole dining room, and the candlestick is not on the sideboard where it was originally."

"Look on the back of the picture and see who took it," said Mrs. Levine.

"The initials are JJ."

"Jeanetta Jones," everyone said at once.

"Those are my initials, but I didn't take that picture," said Jeanetta.

"Who else in the class has those initials?" asked Mrs. Levine.

The room was silent as everyone stopped to think. "I know," said Jeanetta finally. "It's my mother. Her name is Jackie Jones. Remember, she took pictures that day too."

"Of course," said Mrs. Levine. "Jeanetta, please ask your mother tonight if she remembers whether she took this picture when we were in the dining room the first time or the second time."

"Let me see the picture," said Derrick. After studying the photo for a minute, he said, "This must have been taken when we were in the dining room the second time."

"How do you know that?" demanded Janie.

"Easy," said Derrick. "Detective Greeley is not in the picture. We saw him for the first time in the dining room. Then he went with us to the conservatory when we heard the lady scream. When we came back to the dining room to finish the tour, he didn't come with us. He stayed to talk with the fainting lady and her friend. So if the picture had been taken the first time we were in the dining room, Detective Greeley would have been in the picture."

"Great thinking!" exclaimed Mrs. Levine. "That goes to prove that sometimes what you don't see is as important as what you do see. Let's talk some more after lunch."

When the other photographs were examined, they did not reveal good news. There were several close-up shots of the candlestick in front of the mirror. Maria and Debra had both taken these to see what would happen if they took a picture of a mirror. Then there was a picture of the whole class in the dining room with the candlestick. Unfortunately that photo also showed a tall figure in a gray sweatshirt with a hand reaching toward the candlestick. It could only have been Steven.

Lamar looked as sad as he felt when Mrs. Levine handed him the picture. "Ask Steven about this tonight. Even though this picture looks incriminating, I'm sure he has an innocent explanation."

"What's 'incriminating' mean?" asked Janie.

"It means that the picture makes Steven look guilty. But like I said, I'm sure Steven will have an explanation for us. Lamar, did you ask Steven when he first noticed something pulling on his pocket?"

"Yes, I did. He said that he wasn't sure because he kept feeling things the whole time we were at the Eastman House. It was so crowded that people kept bumping into him. Then he caught his pocket on Mr. Eastman's desk when someone pushed him against it. But he thinks that he really started to feel something heavy in his pocket when we were standing by the back door and getting ready to leave."

"Let's summarize what we have found out today," said Mrs. Levine. "If the candlestick was in the dining room the first time we were in it but not there the second time, what can we conclude?"

"The candlestick must have been taken while we were all in the conservatory looking at the fainting lady," said Janie.

"I think you're right, Janie. Let's write that on the FACTS side of our chart," said Mrs. Levine. "Now, if the candlestick was taken while we were all in the conservatory, who could have taken it?"

"Everyone seemed to be in the conservatory," said Lamar.

"Yeah. Everyone ran to see the fainting lady," added Derrick.

"But someone could have sneaked back into the dining room when we were all watching the lady in the conservatory. Isn't that true, Mrs. Levine?" said Janie.

"Unfortunately it is. Mildred created quite a distraction. I don't like what I'm thinking. Suppose she fainted on purpose to give an accomplice time to steal the candlestick?"

"Could somebody do that?" said Jeanetta at the same time that Janie said, "What's an accomplice?"

"Don't be dumb," said Derrick, looking at both girls with disgust. "An accomplice is someone who helps you in a crime, and haven't you ever seen Michael Jordan fake an injury to stall for time?"

"I guess you forgot that we don't use the 'd' word in this class, Derrick," corrected Mrs. Levine. "But I agree with you. People have been known to pretend to be sick before. As a matter of fact, right in this classroom there seems to be an awful lot of sickness just after I say, 'Open your books for math.'" She glanced around the room as several people quickly averted their eyes to the floor.

"But that's another matter, and we're here to discuss suspects. So we're back to the original question. Who are the suspects? Think about that overnight, and we'll discuss it some more tomorrow."

When the last student was gone, Mrs. Levine brought out another big sheet of poster board. In large capital letters she wrote the word SUSPECTS at the top. Wouldn't her students be surprised to see whose name she wrote directly underneath it?

Chapter 18

The next morning Mrs. Levine planted herself directly in front of her desk. She wanted a perfect view of her students' faces as they entered and saw the new wall chart. It didn't take long, as first one student and then another stopped in their tracks and looked at the wall with their mouths open. There on the chart in neat letters under the word SUSPECTS was written the name Audrey Levine.

Finally Derrick spoke. "Aw, Miz Levine, you're not telling us that you took the candlestick, are you?"

Before Mrs. Levine could answer, other students found their tongues and said what they were thinking.

"You didn't do it, Mrs. Levine."

"We know it wasn't you, Mrs. Levine."

"Why'd you put your own name up there?"

"Did you write your name by mistake?"

Jeanetta, who had been listening to everyone's comments, smiled slyly and then spoke. "I think I know why Mrs. Levine put her own name up there."

"So tell us, smartypants," said Derrick.

"It's too early in the morning for this bickering," said

Facts

The Eastman House was very crowded yesterday.
There were many colorful things to look at.
A lady in a purple blazer fainted in the Conservatory.
Detective Greeley left the dining room to help her.
The candlestick was on the sideboard in the dining room in front of the mirror.
There are no fingerprints on the candlestick.
The candlestick must have been taken while we were all in the conservatory looking at the fainting lady.

Questions

Did another student take the candlestick and put it in Steven's pocket?

How did the candlestick get into Steven's pocket?

When was the candlestick put into Steven's pocket?

Suspects

Audrey Levine
Detective Greeley
Ms. Hamilton
Mildred, her friend Helen
Ladies in purple blazers
Ladies in white blazers
Mrs. Whitman

Mrs. Levine. "Go ahead, Jeanetta. I'm interested in what you have to say."

"Well, I started thinking about suspects last night like Mrs. Levine asked us to do. By the way, my mother did take that picture the second time we were in the dining room. Anyway, I realized that if the candlestick was taken while we were all in the conservatory watching Detective Greeley and Mildred the fainting lady, then anyone who was in Eastman House that day could have done it. While we were all watching the stuff in the conservatory, someone could have gone back into the dining room and stolen the candlestick. Mrs. Levine put her own name on the list of suspects to remind us that a detective has to have an open mind. Even people who look innocent are sometimes guilty."

"And people who look guilty are sometimes innocent," chimed in Janie, who had just gotten her friend's point.

"Exactly," said Mrs. Levine. "Jeanetta, you did a marvelous job of explaining why I put my name first on the list of suspects. Unless any of you can swear that you had your eyes on me every minute at Eastman House and can swear without a doubt that I didn't take the candlestick, it will have to remain there." As she spoke these words she scanned the room for any sure faces. All she saw were signs of doubt.

"But Mrs. Levine, you didn't take it, did you?" asked Reinaldo.

"No, I didn't. But my name will stay on the list. And remember, guilty people sometimes lie."

I know that, thought Derrick. Aloud he said, "Does

that mean that we have to put Detective Greeley's name on the list too?"

"Yes," insisted Jeanetta as Mrs. Levine nodded in agreement. "And let's not forget our docent Ms. Hamilton or Mildred the fainting lady or her friend Helen."

"How about the ladies in the purple blazers?" said Reinaldo, getting into the spirit of the debate.

"And the white blazers," added Lamar.

"And how about Mrs. Levine's friend, Mrs. Whitman?" chimed in Tomas.

"Well, we have a great list of suspects, but that really hasn't helped us much, has it?" sighed (only a one on the scale) Mrs. Levine as she put down her marking pen.

"At least we think we know when the candlestick was taken from the dining room. Tomorrow let's focus on when and how it got into Steven's pocket."

Chapter 19

Wednesday's lessons were well under way when there was a knock on the door of Room 217 and in walked Steven. The kids all gaped in silence as Mrs. Levine rushed over to welcome him into the room. She was the only one not totally surprised by Steven's appearance, although when she had spoken with him the night before, she was not at all sure that he would show up today.

"We're glad you're here, Steven. We'd like you to explain this photograph from George Eastman House. Maybe looking at it and other pictures will jog your memory so that we can find out what really happened that day."

The surprised students were still staring when Derrick found his tongue and called out, "Hey, Steven!" With those words the tension in the room dissolved and everyone called out a greeting.

"Yo, Steven."

"Hi, Steven."

"What's goin' on, Steven?"

Steven pulled the incriminating photo that Lamar had brought home out of his pocket. "Yeah, this is me reaching out for the candlestick. The kids ahead of me had bumped up against that dresser it was sitting on and I thought it was gonna fall off. I shoulda just kept my hands in my pockets. And I didn't steal no candlestick."

"Of course you didn't, Steven. We just need to be able to prove it."

At that moment Jeanetta jumped out of her seat screaming, "I've got it! I've got it! I've got it!"

All eyes looked at Jeanetta in disbelief. Jeanetta, the model student, never raised her voice and never, ever jumped out of her seat.

"This must be important," said Mrs. Levine. "Come up here and tell us what you have."

"He didn't do it. He really didn't do it," was all that Jeanetta could say.

"If you're talking about Steven, we know that, but we need proof."

"But I have proof," insisted Jeanetta. "Just look at this picture. I was flipping through my pictures again when Steven said that he should have kept his hands in his pockets. I took this photo in the back hallway just before we left Eastman House. I had one picture left and wanted to finish the roll. Steven has one hand in his pocket, but if you look closely, you'll see that he also has both hands crossed in front of him. How can that be? It has to be someone else's hand in his pocket—someone with a gray sleeve just like Steven."

"Let me see!"

"Let me see!"

"Let me see!"

Everyone wanted to look at Jeanetta's photo at once, but Mrs. Levine stepped in to say, "Steven needs to see this first."

Steven stared so long and hard at the picture that it seemed he would burn a hole in it. Finally he handed the picture back to Jeanetta and turned away so the kids would not see the tears running down his face in relief.

"Well, it can't be one of the ladies in the purple blazers," said Janie.

Steven wiped his eyes with the sleeve of his sweat-shirt and turned back to face the class. "Look at the feet," he said in a whisper.

Jeanetta looked again and there it was. Barely sticking out from behind Steven's dingy sneaker was the bright red toe of a lady's pump.

"MS. HAMILTON, THE DOCENT—SHE DID IT!" screamed Jeanetta.

Mrs. Levine quickly took the picture to the computer and scanned it. Before anyone could ask what she was doing, she had enlarged the photo and printed out twenty-five color copies so everyone could look at once. There in black and white and gray and red was the needed evidence. It hadn't been detected earlier because the gray of Ms. Hamilton's jacket was almost exactly the same color as the gray of Steven's sweatshirt.

Room 217 erupted into loud shouts and wild applause—so much so that it brought Mr. Coley running from his office, which was directly below.

"I'll let Jeanetta explain this to you," said Mrs. Levine as she handed Mr. Coley one of the blown-up pictures. "I must go call Mr. Levine," she cried as she raced to the phone.

"I don't want to be a wet blanket," said Mr. Coley. "But this picture does not prove that Ms. Hamilton took the candlestick either. All we see is what looks like her hand in Steven's pocket. I know it looks suspicious, but I'm not sure it proves anything. Steven, I believe you're innocent. We just need to pursue this further."

The jubilant atmosphere quickly turned to gloom as everyone thought about what Mr. Coley had said. That was still the mood when Mr. Levine arrived a few minutes later.

"I came as soon as I could," he said, rushing in the door. "Let me see that picture." He spent almost as much time as Steven had, looking at the original photo, looking at the enlargement, and then back at the original photo again.

"I think you've got something here, Jeanetta," he finally said. "Let me go visit my friend Sergeant O'Brian on the police force. He'll know what to do." And out he rushed as fast as he had rushed in.

The time dragged in Room 217 after that. Steven accepted Mrs. Levine's offer to spend the day with them to help the time go by faster, but the hands of the clock seemed to be moving in slow motion when they moved at all, and no one called with any news.

Chapter 20

The next morning Mrs. Levine, Mr. Levine, Steven, and Principal Coley all walked into Room 217 together. At least the adults walked into the room. Steven sort of bounced into the room, the noise from his portable CD player leaking out of the headphones. The fact that Steven was back to blaring his music was a good sign.

"Well, students, we have good news," Mrs. Levine was beaming. "I'll let Mr. Levine give you the details," she said as she walked to her desk and sat down. Mr. Coley took a seat in the back of the room. Steven pulled up a chair and draped himself over it backwards. After a look from Mrs. Levine, he turned off the music.

"When I left here yesterday I told you all that I was going to see my friend Sergeant O'Brian at the police department," began Mr. Levine, "and that's exactly what I did. After looking at Jeanetta's photo, he was at least convinced that he should investigate Docent Hamilton a little further. He let me accompany him back to the George Eastman House where we spoke to Kathy Connor, the Curator. After explaining the situation and showing the picture, Ms. Connor opened up her personnel records to Sergeant O'Brian. She even gave the officer Ms. Hamilton's name tag so that he could lift her fingerprints."

"Oh, cool," said Derrick. "I always wanted to see how the cops check for fingerprints."

"What was even cooler, Derrick, was what happened when Sergeant O'Brian ran the fingerprints through the police computer. It turns out that Ms. Hamilton is not Ms. Hamilton after all. Her real name is Elizabeth (Betty) Bronkowski. She's wanted for questioning about some museum thefts in New York and Chicago. She has eluded police several times by moving and changing her identity. Nobody thought to look for her in a smaller city like Rochester, New York. I guess she realized that too, and that's why she came here."

"Way cool," said Derrick.

"She's a real crook?" asked Janie.

"Yes, Janie, she's a real crook, and I haven't gotten to the best part yet, Derrick. Last night Sergeant O'Brian and his partner paid a surprise visit to Ms. Hamilton's—I mean Bronkowski's—apartment. She lives on East Avenue just down the street from the Eastman House. He wouldn't let me go with him, but he called afterwards to tell me the details.

"According to Sergeant O'Brian, when he addressed Ms. Hamilton as Ms. Bronkowski, she started to get very nervous. She insisted she knew nothing about a Ms. Bronkowski and kept repeating that she wasn't the one in Jeanetta's picture. She said that lots of women wear gray and have red shoes.

"All of a sudden her phone rang. When the police officers turned to look at the ringing phone, she bolted out of the apartment and took off for the stairs. Unfortunately for her, she was wearing those same red high-heeled shoes from the photo and tripped on the third step going down. She landed at the bottom of the stairs, which is where Sergeant O'Brian picked her up. His partner called for an ambulance while he hand-cuffed her and read her her rights.

"As the attendants carried Ms. Bronkowski out to the waiting ambulance, she yelled, 'I'll sue you for false arrest you ---------.'" A glance at Mrs. Levine had told him that he should not repeat everything that the angry woman had said."

"Is she dead?" asked Jeanetta.

"Did she have a gun?" asked Derrick

"Actually, she will be fine, and she didn't have a gun. She broke her left leg, bruised her ribs, and got a deep gash on her forehead that needed stitches, but she will have lots of time to recuperate in jail. Sergeant O'Brian went back to her apartment with a search warrant while she was in the emergency room and found a stolen painting hanging right in plain sight on her bedroom wall. It was a Cezanne taken from the Museum of Modern Art last year in New York City. Apparently Ms. Bronkowski liked it so much she couldn't bear to fence it. She thought that the hicks here in Rochester wouldn't recognize it."

"What do you mean she was going to fence it? The picture wasn't outside," said Justina.

"Fencing is a slang term. It means she was going to sell it to another crook who would sell it for her."

"What was she going to do with the candlestick?" asked Janie.

"Nobody knows for sure, since she's not talking, but the police think she was just waiting for a crowded day at the George Eastman House to steal something. When Helen fainted and everyone was distracted, Ms. Bronkowski saw an opportunity and took the candlestick. The police think she was going to hide it in the bushes outside the back door and come back for it at night. She didn't expect Detective Greeley to miss it so soon. When he hollered for everyone to stop, she knew right away what was wrong. She didn't want to be caught with the candlestick and didn't have time to take it outside, so she stuck it in Steven's pocket. He happened to be in the wrong place at the wrong time."

The room was silent as the students tried to absorb everything that Mr. Levine said.

Finally Derrick said, "That makes sense to me." Twenty-four heads nodded in agreement.

"So now what happens to Steven?" Jeanetta asked.

"That's the best part. Although the police can't prove that Ms. Hamilton, or Bronkowski, or whatever her name is, took the candlestick, they're convinced that she did. The charges against Steven have been dropped, and he is a free man. Your photograph, Jeanetta, saved the day."

With that, Derrick, Lamar, Janie, and Reinaldo ran over to Jeanetta, grabbed her out of her seat, hoisted her on their shoulders, and carried her around the classroom.

Mrs. Levine and Mr. Coley didn't even seem to mind. In fact, they were the ones cheering the loudest as the queen and her subjects rounded the coat closets and stopped in front of the chalkboard after the third lap around the room.

Steven slouched out of his seat and edged over to Jeanetta. Since she was still on the kids' shoulders, Jeanetta and Steven were eye to eye. Steven touched Jeanetta's shoulder and said, "Thanks, Jeanetta."

Jeanetta blushed and said, "You're welcome, Steven. I just couldn't let Lamar's brother go to jail."

It was Lamar's turn to blush, and he said, "Thanks, Jeanetta, you're the greatest."

"This calls for a party," said Mr. Coley. "Call up Pizza Hut, Mrs. Levine. The pizza's on me." He walked back to his office with the students' cheers ringing in his ears.

"Now boys and girls," said Mrs. Levine, "do you see how important photography is? It even helped us solve a crime."

Derrick felt another lecture coming on, but even Mrs. Levine knew when enough had been said. She ended her remarks with one last thought. "I wonder what George Eastman would think about this!"

Author's Note

George Eastman House is a National Historic Landmark located at 900 East Avenue in the heart of Rochester, New York. The house and gardens have been restored to their original elegance, reflecting Eastman's life in the first quarter of the twentieth century. The twelve-and-a-half-acre estate also houses the International Museum of Photography and Film. The house, gardens, and photography museum are all open to the public.

Kathy Connor has been the curator of George Eastman House since the position was created in November of 1989. Aside from Mr. Eastman, Mayor Johnson, and Curator Connor, all of the characters and events in this book are strictly fictional. As far as I know, George Eastman did not receive a candlestick from King George V.

About the Author

Sally Valentine is a native Rochesterian, who has been both a student and a teacher in the Rochester City School District. After teaching math for twenty-five years, she is now off on a tangent of writing. *Theft at George Eastman House* is the second book in a series of books she is writing about the places and people of Rochester. Her first book, *The Ghost of the Charlotte Lighthouse* was published by North Country Books in 2006. Both books are part of North Country's New York State Adventure series. Check out her Web site: www.RochesterAuthor.com. Teachers who would like to use the books as part of their Social Studies curriculum may download student worksheets for each book. Sally is currently working on her next novel, *What Stinks? An Adventure in Highland Park*, and also a book of poems about New York State entitled *There Are No Buffalo in Buffalo*.